# Stock Cars

BY JACK DAVID

TORQUE™

BELLWETHER MEDIA • MINNEAPOLIS, MN

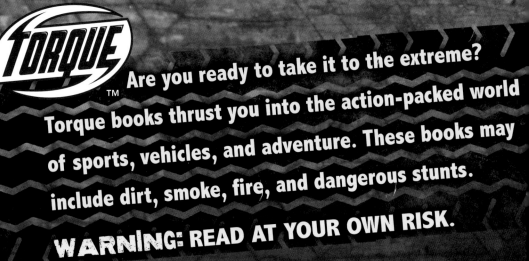

Are you ready to take it to the extreme? Torque books thrust you into the action-packed world of sports, vehicles, and adventure. These books may include dirt, smoke, fire, and dangerous stunts.

WARNING: READ AT YOUR OWN RISK.

This edition first published in 2008 by Bellwether Media.

No part of this publication may be reproduced in whole or in part without written permission of the publisher. For information regarding permission, write to Bellwether Media Inc., Attention: Permissions Department, Post Office Box 19349, Minneapolis, MN 55419.

Library of Congress Cataloging-in-Publication Data

David, Jack, 1968-
  Stock cars / Jack David.
     p. cm. --  (Torque--cool rides)
  Summary: "Full color photography accompanies engaging information about Stock Cars. The combination of high-interest subject matter and light text is intended for students in grades 3 through 7"--Provided by publisher.
  Includes bibliographical references and index.
  ISBN-13: 978-1-60014-153-9 (hardcover : alk. paper)
  ISBN-10: 1-60014-153-6 (hardcover : alk. paper)
  1. Stock cars (Automobiles)--Juvenile literature. 2. Stock car racing--Juvenile literature. I. Title.

TL236.28.D38 2008
629.228--dc22

2007040567

# Contents

# What Is a Stock Car?

Stock cars are stronger, faster, and louder versions of regular road cars. The first stock cars were all factory-built. Modern stock cars are still based on factory cars. They are also built to suit the demands of modern racing.

Stock cars are race cars. The racing is tight and fast in a stock car competition. Forty-three cars speed at 200 miles (322 kilometers) per hour. They're only inches apart. Drivers bump and grind at amazing speeds as they battle for the lead. Stock car racing is truly a sport on the edge.

# Fast FaCt

The largest stock car track is Talladega Superspeedway. One lap around the track is more than 2.5 miles (4 kilometers)!

# Stock Car History

Stock car racing began in the 1920s. Cars were just becoming widely available to the public. People liked to race them on dirt tracks. They worked on the cars to make them faster.

Stock car racing changed forever in 1947. A man named Bill France formed the National Association for Stock Car Automobile Racing (NASCAR). NASCAR gave drivers and tracks a set of rules to follow. It also set up racing classes. The sport's popularity soared.

The most successful driver in NASCAR history is Richard Petty. From 1958 to 1992, Petty won 200 races and seven championships.

# Stock Car Parts

Everything inside the body of a stock car is stronger and more powerful than a normal car. Body panels fit over the **chassis** of a stock car. The chassis is made of very strong metal tubing.

An extra set of metal bars sits around the driver. This **roll cage** protects the driver during crashes.

The **suspension system** connects the wheels to the chassis. It includes springs and shock absorbers.

Smooth tires called **slicks** give stock cars the best grip on paved tracks.

Stock cars have powerful **V8 engines**. A V8 engine is made up of eight fuel-burning **cylinders** arranged in the shape of a V. The powerful engines produce about 750 **horsepower**. That's about three times more powerful than a normal car engine!

## Fast Fact

Bill Elliot holds the speed record for a stock car. In 1987, he did a lap at Talladega at an average of 213 miles (343 kilometers) per hour.

15

The **drive train** transfers the engine's power to the wheels. It contains a set of gears. Drivers change gears with a shifter. They start in first gear. They work up to fourth gear as they gain speed.

# Stock Cars in Action

NASCAR races are huge events. Some races draw hundreds of thousands of fans. The races can be 600 miles (966 kilometers) long!

Drivers work hard to compete in a race.
They **draft** behind other cars to gain extra speed.
Drivers also have to make **pit stops**. In a pit stop,
the driver goes to the pit area. That driver's team
rushes out to add fuel and change the tires.
This usually takes 15 seconds or less! Then the
driver speeds back onto the track.
Everyone wants to be the first
one across the finish line.

## Fast Fact

Race winners like to show off for the crowd. Many of them do burnouts— they spin the tires to create huge clouds of smoke.

# Glossary

**chassis**—the metal frame of a stock car

**cylinder**—a hollow chamber inside an engine in which fuel is burned to create power

**draft**—to closely follow another car in order to reduce wind resistance

**drive train**—the part of a car that transfers power from the engine to the wheels

**horsepower**—a unit for measuring the power of an engine

**pit stop**—a time during a race when a team adds fuel to the car, changes its tires, and makes adjustments or minor repairs

**roll cage**—a set of strong metal bars that surrounds the driver and protects him during crashes

**slicks**—smooth racing tires

**suspension system**—the system of springs and shock absorbers that connects a stock car's chassis to its wheels

**V8 engine**—an engine with eight fuel-burning cylinders arranged in the shape of a V

# To Learn More

## AT THE LIBRARY

Armentrout, David and Patricia. *Tony Stewart: In the Fast Lane*. Vero Beach, Fla.: Rourke, 2007

Bullard, Lisa. *Stock Cars*. Minneapolis, Minn.: Lerner, 2004.

Doeden, Matt. NASCAR: *Under the Hood*. Mankato, Minn.: Capstone, 2008.

## ON THE WEB

Learning more about stock cars is as easy as 1, 2, 3.

1. Go to www.factsurfer.com

2. Enter "stock cars" into search box.

3. Click the "Surf" button and you will see a list of related web sites.

With factsurfer.com, finding more information is just a click away.

# Index

The images in this book are reproduced through the courtesy of: Rusty Jarrett/
Stringer/Getty Images, front cover, pp. 13, 17; Darrell Ingham/Getty Images, p.
5; John Sommers II/Stringer/Getty Images, p. 6; Robert Laberge/Stringer/Getty
Images, p. 7; Southern Photo Archives/Alamy, p. 9; Todd Warshaw/Stringer/Getty
Images, pp. 10-11; Todd Taulman, p. 14; Jamie Squire/Getty Images, p. 15; Jason
Smith/Stringer/Getty Images, p. 16; Jeff Bottari/Stringer/Getty Images, p. 18; Chris
Graythen/Stringer/Getty Images, pp. 20-21.